Through Sand, Snow and Steam

HISTORICAL SHORT STORIES

Contents

The Escape

by Ian Serraillier

illustrated by Peter Davies

The Foreigner

by Theresa Breslin

illustrated by Kathryn Baker

Kindertransport

by Dennis Hamley

illustrated by Claire Fletcher

PEARSON
Longman

The Escape
from *The Silver Sword*
by Ian Serraillier

First I must tell of Joseph Balicki and what
happened to him in the prison camp of Zakyna.

The prison camp that the Nazis sent him to
was in the mountains of South Poland. A few
wooden huts clung to the edge of the bleak
hillside. Day and night the wind beat down
upon them. For five months of the year snow
lay thick upon the ground. It gave a coating of
white fur to the twelve-foot double fence of wire
that surrounded the clearing. In stormy weather
it blew into the bare huts. There was no comfort
in Zakyna.

The camp was crowded with prisoners. Most
of them were Poles, but there were some Czechs,
Hungarians and a few Russians, too. Each hut
held about a hundred and twenty – yet it was

hardly big enough
for more than
forty. They passed
the time playing
chess, sewing,
reading, fighting for old
newspapers or cigarette
stumps, quarrelling, shouting. At mealtimes they
huddled round to eat their cabbage and potato
soup. It was the same for every meal. For
drinking they had warm water with breadcrumbs
in it – the Nazi guards called it coffee.

Few had the strength or the spirit to escape.
Several prisoners had got away. Those that were
not caught and sent back died of exposure in
the mountains.

But Joseph was determined to escape. During
the first winter he was too ill to try. He would
sit around the hut, thinking of his family and

staring at the photos
of them that he had
been allowed to keep.
He would think of his
school in Warsaw.

When the Nazis came, they
had taken away the Polish
textbooks and made him
teach in German. They
had hung pictures of
Hitler in all the
classrooms. Once, Joseph
had turned the picture of
Hitler's face to the wall.
Someone had reported this
to the Nazis.

Then the Nazi storm troops
had come for Joseph in the middle
of the night and bundled him off to Zakyna.
They had left Margrit and the three children
behind. How he longed to see them again!

During the summer his health mended, but
the number of guards was doubled.

The following winter he was ill again. He
decided to wait till early spring, when the snow
was beginning to melt.

Very carefully he laid his plans.

It was no use thinking of cutting the wire
fence. There was a trip-line inside the double

fence, and anyone who crossed it would be shot. There was only one way out – the way the guards went, through the gate and past the guardhouse. His idea was to disguise himself as one of them and follow them as they went off duty. But how was he to get hold of the uniform?

At the back of each block was an unheated hut known as 'the cooler'. It had three or four cells to which prisoners were sent to 'cool off'. In winter you could freeze to death there. In spring, with a bit of luck, you might survive a night or two.

One March day, during the morning hut

inspection, he flicked a paper pellet at the guard. It stung him behind the ear and made him turn round. Within five minutes Joseph was in a cell in 'the cooler'.

For two days he stamped up and down, to keep himself warm. He clapped his arms against his sides. He dared not lie down in case he dropped off to sleep and never woke again. Twice a day a guard brought him food. For the rest of the time he was alone.

On the evening of the third day the guard came as usual. Joseph crouched down on the floor at the back of his tiny cell. He had a smooth round stone and a catapult in his hands. He  had made the catapult from twigs and the elastic sides of his boots. His eyes were fixed on the flap in the door. Joseph waited. He heard the key grate in the rusty lock. Heavy boots clumped across the floor towards his cell.

Joseph drew back the elastic. He heard the padlock on the flap being unlocked. The flap slid aside.

The guard had not seen Joseph when the stone struck him and knocked him down.

Joseph must act quickly, before the guard

came to his senses. He knew the guard kept his bunch of keys in his pocket. He must get hold of them.

He took a hook and line from under his bed. He had made the line by cutting thin strips from his blanket. The hook was a bent four-inch nail that he had smuggled in from his hut.

After several attempts, the hook caught in the top button of the guard's coat. He tugged at the line and drew the guard up towards him ... higher and higher.

Suddenly the line snapped. The guard fell back. The hook was lost.

Joseph had one spare hook, that was all.

He tried again. This time the cotton broke and the button went spinning across the floor.

He had begun to despair when he saw
the keys. They were lying on the floor.
They had been shaken out of a
pocket when the guard fell.

Quickly Joseph fished for the ring
of keys and hauled it up. A few
moments later he was kneeling beside
the body, stripping off the uniform.
There was no time to lose. He could hear the
guards shouting outside.

Joseph felt warm in the guard's uniform. The
coat reached to his ankles. The fur cap had flaps
for covering his ears. He smiled to himself as he
locked the guard in the freezing cell. Then,
turning up his collar, he went out into the bitter
night.

He walked through the snow. In dark
shadows behind the huts he hid until the
trumpet sounded the change of guard.

Hundreds of times he had watched the
soldiers of the guard fall in and march out of
camp. He had memorized every order, every
movement. It seemed to him quite natural now
to be lining up with the others.

"Anything to report?" the officer asked each of them in turn.

"All correct, sir," they answered.

"All correct, sir," said Joseph in his best German.

"Guard, dismiss!" said the officer.

Joseph followed the other soldiers out – out of the gate and into freedom. It seemed too good to be true.

Some of the soldiers stopped outside the guardhouse to gossip.

"Where are you going?" one of them called.

"Shangri La," he muttered. It was the soldiers' name for the nightclub in the village where they sometimes spent their off-duty times. Without looking behind him, he walked on.

The Foreigner
by Theresa Breslin

Mongolia is a huge country in eastern Asia, lying between Russia and China. It is known as the land of blue sky and is made up of high mountains, wide belts of grasslands, and great deserts. The following is a story from one of the tribespeople who lived there in the thirteenth century ...

So, I will tell you now of the things that happened to me, Lenek, in the eleventh year of my life, when my father was khan of one of the horse tribes of Mongolia.

It was late in that year before we set out for winter camp. The cattle fed well in the grasslands and the mares had fattened and foaled under the hot sun of summer. Our riders had picked out the best from the wild herds of

khan: ruler

horses that roam the land. My father was pleased with the work. I heard him tell my mother that, when the time came to trade, we would earn enough to buy food to see us all through the harsh winter months.

We knew that it was time to take down the tents when the days grew shorter and the early morning dew sparkled with frost. One day a great number of geese flew over us, honking loudly to each other. We watched the long V-shape heading towards the south-west, and saw that soon we too must move on.

The small storage tents and the larger family gers were taken down and loaded into the wagons. Household goods were packed on the camels. Our birds of prey, livestock and horses were gathered together. All was made ready to leave. The evening before we departed my father talked with the shaman and made

offerings to the spirits. To journey towards the mountains our caravan had to cross the edge of the Great Desert. And it was there that I found the foreigner and nearly lost my life.

This desert is not flat, nor is it all sand. There are vast areas of rock, and then miles and miles of soft hills and hollows of sand. Nothing lives in the sand belt. A traveller may journey for many days without seeing even an insect. The oases are spaced far apart and my father was

gers: family tents
shaman: holy man

13

not happy to be crossing even a short stretch of this desert.

As the days passed, the double humps of our camels began to shrink and hang loose, and they were bellowing and biting out with rage at seeing the horses given water from our stores. But the trade for the horses is what we live on during the winter, so only they and the young children and the elderly were allowed to drink their fill. We went onwards slowly in the heat of the day, and at night round the campfires we told stories of the spirits who live in the desert. The storytellers warned the young ones to beware of hearing men laughing or women singing, or the sweet low murmur of a little stream. They said, "You will wander off to look, and you will be lost forever."

We all huddled closer to each other as we settled around our campfires. And at night, before I fell asleep, I would put my hands over my ears to shut out any noise. But one night in the stillness I thought that I heard a spirit whispering to me. "Lenek. Come away. Come away, Lenek, come away."

I cried
out in my
sleep and
raised myself up in
my bed. My father spoke
to me in a soft voice and I cuddled in
once more. But I did not sleep. I lay awake and
gazed up at the stars.

At dawn, I heard a noise like the ripple of the
grass, like wind on water, coming nearer,
growing louder. Our dogs began to growl, and I
called out again to my father. He awoke, and at
once leaped to his feet and looked
out into the desert.

"Storm! Storm!" He shouted
the warning. "Sandstorm!
Sandstorm!"

We rushed to protect
our beasts, our goods
and ourselves as the
racing dust swept
down upon us.
The earth itself
moved and spun,

and we were blinded and choked as we struggled to shelter.

After the storm had passed the world had altered. Where there had been a valley was now a plain, a hill had become a smooth hollow.

That morning, before we set out, my father checked the ropes linking the camels together. He told every person to tie their own water bottle to their belt and not take it off.

For most of that day I rode at the front beside my father with his great eagle perched on his arm. From when I was little my father said that my eyes were almost as sharp as his eagle's, and I liked to ride, hunting with him. In the later part of the day, nearly a quarter of a mile away to the east, I saw a small shape.

"Marmoset!" I cried and pointed.

My father spoke to the eagle and it took off, searching. But it returned without a strike.

"Your eyes have played you false this time little one," my father teased me. He held up his arm and the bird flew to him.

I stopped and pretended to check my saddle. I was annoyed to be mistaken. I rode back to the end of the caravan, but the herders had their hands full keeping the line and had no time for me.

In a few minutes I again passed the place where I thought I had seen the marmoset. I screwed my eyes against the sun and it seemed to me that the shape had changed, become larger. Was it a horse, fallen in the sand? I glanced at the riders in front and decided to say nothing. I did not want to be wrong twice in one day. I slowed the pace of my horse and then, quietly, so that no one would notice, I slipped away. I would only be gone five or ten minutes at the most. That's what I thought.

* * * * *

It was a young man! He was about sixteen years old and lay with his face half in the sand.

His body was lifeless. I decided to leave him and return quickly to the caravan. The long train was still in sight, moving steadily on. I looked down again. He was breathing!

I dismounted and went closer. He was a foreigner, not one of us. His eyes were strange circles in his face, enclosed with rounded lids that did not slope across as normal. I helped him sit up. His eyelids fluttered and he muttered words in a language I did not know. I tried to give him water from my bottle but he spilled more than he drank. It would be best, I decided, to return to the caravan and bring help. I left my water bottle beside him, remounted and looked to the horizon. The caravan with all my people had disappeared.

My heart jumped. But I was certain of their direction so I kicked my horse and rode on after them. After fifteen minutes I knew that I was lost. I tried not to become alarmed. I climbed on my horse's back and stood as high as I could. In every direction stretched sand, endless sand. The sun was low. Night would come quickly, and with it, bitter cold. If I survived this night then the next day's heat would scorch me. I had no water. I would die within a day or so.

I resolved to try to find the foreigner and my water bottle. I turned to look the way I had come. The sand had covered my tracks. I swallowed and swallowed to calm myself. I looked at the sun, and at the moon, which was already in the sky, and tried to remember their position when I had been riding. And then I leaned low along the neck of my horse and I spoke to her. I had ridden my horse as soon as I could walk.

"You must help me," I whispered in her ear.

The sun was burning orange when I saw the little hillock in the sand that was the man. I sa his shoulders slump a he realised that I retur alone. There was no water left in the bottle.

I made the best preparations I could for night, urging my horse to lie beside us for warmth. In the early part of the night we dozed and then awoke shaking with cold. By the light of the moon I could see the young man's eyes staring. Suddenly he gave a start and tilted his head to one side, listening. A terrible fear entered my soul. The spirits of the desert were calling to him. I had to think of something to divert his attention, and mine. I began to talk to him but he shook his head. He did not know my language. I said some words in Chinese and he seemed to understand. So in a mixture of both languages I began to talk. I told him who I was, and of our tribe and where we came from. That we were going to winter camp by way of the trading post at Bataar. There we would sell the horses we had bred and tamed. On and on through the night I spoke, telling him of how the Great Khan needed many, many horses for his armies and post service. How each cavalry warrior has at least nine horses, so that he has a fresh mount each day and his other horses may rest. Thus the army can cover tremendous distances and is always fresh for any attack. Thousands of horses are needed for the messengers of the Great Khan. The riders are tied into the saddle. They wear leather straps with bells that ring out as they ride so that the next post station can hear them coming and have new horses ready. This way they can cover over two hundred miles in one day. I talked and talked and made the young man pay attention to me.

When morning came I was exhausted. The sun rose in the sky. By now I would have been missed. Would my father stop the caravan to come and look for me? Even if he did, he would not know where to search. I looked then at my horse and I decided to free her so that she might survive. It was also in my mind that if she managed to regain the caravan, then she might bring them to me.

The foreigner and I sat together through the day. As the sun grew hotter I wanted to lie down in the sand, but the foreigner would not let me. We leaned against each other back to back. My throat was parched. I imagined I saw green trees growing all around us. I closed my eyes. I did not see the huge shadow of the bird in the sky above us. But the foreigner saw it and let out a cry of dread, believing it to be a vulture come to eat us alive. It was not. It was my father's eagle.

* * * * *

As soon as I was able to stand my father cuffed me, hugged me, then cuffed me some more.

"You are lucky that your horse has more intelligence than its owner and was able to guide us to this place," he shouted. "Never, never leave the caravan. If you do so another time, I will not turn back for you."

When I was permitted to speak, I asked about the foreigner.

"I do not know what land he is from," said my father. "He must be from beyond the Empire of the Great Khan."

At the trading post we got a good price for the horses and were able to buy lots of food – salt blocks and spices, oil, dates and nuts. My father spoke of the foreigner to the traders, but none of them had heard of any missing traveller.

* * * * *

The wind was blowing keenly from the northern mountains when my father brought us to the place called Khurkhree, which means 'waterfall'.

"This is a good site," my father said. He spread his arms wide, "There is space enough for all our tents and animals, with good winter hunting and fresh water."

Then my father took the first drink of airag, the milk of the mare. His fourth finger he dipped in the bowl and tossed the droplets to the sky, the fire, the wind.

We unrolled the bands of thick felt, wrapped them round the circular-shaped frame of our ger and placed the animal skins on top. The opening is always built to face south and then everything put inside in its own place. My

mother set her loom by the right-hand side of
the door and spread bright rugs upon the floor.
We laid the stranger on a bed near the fire.

A few of the unsold horses we kept. The rest
we turned loose. The winter would claim them
or they would live through. The weak perish.
Thus the herds are protected and kept strong.

That first night, at her loom, my mother
sang. I glanced up and saw that the foreigner's
eyes were open. My mother, following my
look, turned her head. She stopped singing and
said to me, "Make some tea with plenty of salt
in it."

His tongue was still swollen in his mouth,
but he got up and drank. And
after he drank, he spoke in
Chinese. "Thank you,"
he said. "Thank you."

The stones in
the stove
sparked
and

startled him. He stared at the fire and asked, "What are they?"

I replied, "These are the black stones we buy from the traders of the northern hills."

I went to light the butter lamp. When I returned he was kneeling at the stove and had put his hand right into the fire! He yelped in pain but had managed to touch a living coal. He gestured to me, making his eyes wide and raising his eyebrows in surprise, and spoke in his own language, words that I did not understand but I can remember. "Stones that burn," he said. "This is indeed marvellous."

He was very skilful with words. Very few outsiders can speak our language. He was with us for only a short time yet he learned enough that I could understand him. He called his own language Italian. I tried very hard with it but stumbled over even the simplest phrases.

"Your way of saying our words is very clear," I told him.

"In all the lands I travel I learn a few words of each language."

"There are too many," I said. "The Chinese

alone have many thousands of words. I do not think that there can be space inside a person's head for all the words of the world."

He replied, "There is more space inside your head, Lenek, than there are grains of sand in the Great Desert."

The second night, the foreigner told us a story – a story of a city where the streets were made of water. Most of us laughed and did not believe him, but my father did not laugh. He asked the foreigner, "Do families visit each other in this city? Do men trade and women go to market?"

The foreigner said, "Yes, they do."

"How do people travel on these streets of water?" my father asked.

"On boats," said the foreigner. And he drew with a stick in the ground the outline of a narrow boat with a high stern,

where a man stood using a pole to move the boat forward. "Gondola," he said.

My father thought for a minute or two. Then he nodded, and said, "It is possible."

* * * * *

On the third day riders came into our camp. They had been told of the foreigner at the trading post. They were looking for a young man who had gone missing from their caravan during a sandstorm in the Great Desert some days ago. They were important men on their way to the summer palace of the Great Khan at Shangdu. My father feared no one, but I saw his face turn pale as they spoke the name of Kublai Khan.

Two of the men came into our ger. Their names were Nicolo and Matteo. The foreigner embraced them, calling them father and uncle. The men thanked us very courteously and sincerely and said that they would speak of us to the Great Khan.

Before they left the foreigner came to speak to me. "I will not forget thee, Lenek," he said,

"though I travel the
world ten times over. When I return home I will
write of the many marvels I have seen in this
land. Of stones that burn and messengers who
can ride over two hundred miles in one day."

Then he wrote down his name, the name he
had been given by his own people at his birth.
I have it yet, inked on a piece of rough paper he

gave me, with the sign of the Great Kublai Khan at the bottom.

In his language.

By his own hand.

Kindertransport
by Dennis Hamley

What upset Kurt and Inge most was that their parents couldn't come on the platform with them. Kurt was eleven and Inge was six. They were starting a long journey alone – except for two hundred other children.

The station in Berlin was full of smoke and steam from huge railway engines. Soldiers, sailors and airmen crowded the platforms. War had started in Poland and everyone knew it would spread. Gestapo men and SS guards stood, watching everything, missing nothing.

The train that Kurt and Inge and all the other children were being hustled onto was going west, to the Hook of Holland. From there, a ship would take them to England.

Inge was crying already. Kurt couldn't tell his

SS: (Schutz-Staffel) Nazi special police force

sister to be brave and stop it. Other children were crying as well, and Kurt was close to tears himself. The Gestapo had made the parents say their goodbyes hurriedly in the waiting room. The mothers and fathers had clung to their children until they'd been forced apart. When the children were on board, the doors slammed shut and the train moved slowly out of the station. Every wheel beat took them further away from everything they had known since they were born.

The date was 1st September, 1939. The Kindertransports had been leaving for nearly a year, from Berlin, Vienna, Prague and every other big city in Hitler's New Reich. They were trains for children, taking them from the lands where they were born because Hitler's people did not want them.

How did they know they weren't wanted? Because people spat and hissed *Juden* at them in the street. Blond boys from the Hitler Youth beat them up. They weren't allowed to go to school anymore. One dreadful night in 1938 they woke up to find every Jewish shop with its windows smashed – they called it *Kristallnacht*, the night of broken glass. Even worse, some children's fathers were taken away by the SS guards. If they came back, they were pale and thin, with all the fight gone out of them. Sometimes they didn't come back.

A number was hung round Kurt's neck – 126. Inge was number 127. The same numbers were tied to their suitcases. As the train gathered speed, Kurt thought, "It's all true, what they said. Our old lives are over."

There was an awful, cold feeling in his stomach. He had thought today could never happen. Could he bear a new life in a strange, cold country where they spoke a language that he hardly knew? He had started to learn English when he was at school, but that finished when they didn't allow him to go to school anymore. He shuddered.

Inge looked up at him and said, "When will Mummy and Daddy be coming?"

He couldn't tell her what he feared. "Very soon," he said.

Inge smiled for the first time since she had woken up that morning. Kurt felt sad and fearful, because he knew that one day Inge would remember what he said. Then she might not trust him anymore.

"Keep smiling, Inge," he said. "We're going to England. It's not like Hitler's Germany. They want us there. We'll have a wonderful new life." He tried to believe what he said, but the cold in his stomach wouldn't go away.

Yet they were lucky. They'd survived. They'd

got away. "Think about that," he told himself. "Forget everything else."

But as he thought about this new life, he was fearful again. Why were they on this train when so many were left behind? People in England had given money to get them there. Some children were going to live with relatives. But Kurt and Inge had no relatives in England. Their parents had applied to get their children on the train, though they had no idea where they would be living or who with. When Kurt thought of living with strangers the cold feeling in his stomach grew worse.

The train banged on through the dusk. The windows clouded with steam. It was like flying through space, the last living things in the world.

* * * * *

At last they reached the border between Germany and Holland. The train stopped. Nothing happened. Then Inge asked, "Kurt, why are we going backwards?"

It was true. They were moving backwards.

For a sickening moment Kurt thought that the English had changed their minds. Then the train stopped again. The doors burst open. "It's the SS," he whispered.

"*Raus, raus*! Everybody out!" the SS guards shouted. "*Schnell, Schnell*! Quick, quick! Bring your cases."

The children rushed to get out. But Inge stood still, rigid with fear.

"Come on, Inge," said Kurt gently. "We have to go." He tried to take her hand, but her fingers were tight and her arms clamped to her sides. "If we don't do what the SS guards say, they won't let Mummy and Daddy come to England."

She looked up at him. "Really?" she said. "Honestly?"

"Honestly," he said, and felt even worse.

Slowly he brought her out of the train to a brightly lit hall with long tables. They stood there, still and afraid.

"Put your cases on the tables," an SS officer shouted. The SS guards started their work. Every case was ripped open.

A big man in a black uniform tore Inge's case. Clothes and dolls spilled over the table. Another guard, smaller and mean-looking, pulled at Kurt's.

Suddenly, the angry voice of a woman sounded over the noise.

37

"What do you think you are doing?"

There was a sudden hush. The small guard muttered, "It's that Dutch woman again," and went on pulling at Kurt's case. But the big SS guard stopped him.

The SS officer replied politely, "Our duty to the fatherland, ma'am."

"This isn't duty," she snapped. "It's vandalism."

The SS officer said, "Lady, I don't think you like us very much."

"You're right," she replied.

The small guard muttered, "These Dutch. They'll be sorry soon."

The woman left. To Kurt's surprise, the SS officer ordered, "Stop work. Let the children go."

The guards did as he said. The children stuffed their things back into the cases and soon the train was on its way again. They were out of Germany now, passing through a friendly land. They laughed and shouted with relief. Suddenly, the journey seemed happy.

Two hours later, they were at the Hook of Holland, boarding the ship for England. As it moved slowly away from the land, Kurt said to Inge, "We really have left our homes now. Nobody can get us when we're across the sea."

The North Sea was cold and rough. Inge was sick three times. Kurt wanted to be sick too, but he vowed he wouldn't in front of Inge. But as the sun rose over a sparkling sea, they saw a wide, flat land ahead of them.

"Look, Inge. That's England," said Kurt.

As the ship approached the shore they could see villages, fields, trees. Soon the boat was tying up in harbour. The children walked down the gangplank into England, past the men who

checked their papers, then stepped outside.

What a surprise! There was a crowd of people and sudden flashes from the cameras of press photographers. For a moment, Kurt was frightened. Then he said out loud, "No, this is England. They want us."

But he still wasn't quite sure.

The children were put on the train and it set off for London through a land of low hills and trees. In two hours they came to London, to Liverpool Street station.

Soon they were sitting in yet another hall, waiting. Most children were met by relatives, gathered up with kisses by aunts and uncles. Kurt watched with longing in his heart. If only they had relatives in England. After an hour of waiting, only Kurt and Inge were left.

An Englishwoman with a clipboard joined the Transport Leader. She kept looking, first at the lists, then at the two children.

"What are they saying, Kurt?" asked Inge.

"I think the Englishwoman is saying we can't stay here. We have to go to a place called the Refugee Centre," said Kurt.

The Transport Leader came over to them. "Don't worry," he said. "Go with this lady. I have to go back on the next train."

At the Refugee Centre Kurt and Inge waited anxiously. Night came: still the children sat there. Eventually a woman spoke to them. "Come with me," she said. "There's a hostel nearby. I can get you beds there for the night."

She was right. "Come to the Centre first thing in the morning," she said as she paid for their beds.

First thing next morning they were back. It was 3rd September, 1939. Again they waited. At last, the same woman came over to them.

"We've been lucky," she said. "We've found somewhere for you. A family in Birmingham is willing to take two children, so you won't be split up. They sound very nice. Their name is Ferris. I'll put you on the train."

Suddenly there was a hush. Someone had put a wireless on. A man's voice was speaking. It sounded tired and old. When he finished, the wireless was switched off. Nobody spoke.

"What's happening, Kurt?" asked Inge.

"Great Britain is at war with Germany," Kurt answered.

Inge suddenly wailed. "Does this mean Mummy and Daddy can't come to England?"

"Of course not," Kurt replied. "They'll be here soon, you'll see." But deep inside he felt sick. Yet again he hadn't told her the truth and one day she would know.

He didn't have long to feel sad. The woman bustled over and said, "I'll take you to the station."

At the station the woman bought their tickets and said, "There are labels on your cases saying 'Birmingham'. The train doesn't go any further, so you'll be all right, but I've asked the guard to look after you. Mrs Ferris will meet you there."

A whistle blew and the train slowly drew out.

The woman ran along the platform. "Goodbye, Kurt and Inge," she called. "And good luck."

* * * * *

Two hours later, the train drew into Birmingham. Kurt grabbed their cases and Inge's hand, then, when the other passengers had got off, he led her onto the platform. They stood alone, feeling lost.

A jolly-looking woman waved, spread her arms out and half ran towards them. "Welcome to Birmingham, my dears," she cried. "I'm so pleased to see you. Let me take your cases. It won't take long to get home."

She led them to a little blue car parked outside.

She lifted Inge onto the back seat and put the cases in next to her. Kurt sat in the front seat. As Mrs Ferris drove through Birmingham, she said, "Now you can forget all about that nasty old Hitler. You'll be all right now you're in England."

Kurt tried hard to understand her. "But war has started," he said.

"Oh dear, I hoped you didn't know yet. Well, we mustn't let that worry us. We'll win, like we won the last war. Everything will be fine."

"Does that mean Mother and Father will come here soon?"

Mrs Ferris took her hand off the steering wheel and squeezed Kurt's hand. "Oh, Kurt," she said. "I do hope so."

They turned down a pleasant, tree-lined road and into the drive of a semi-detached house. "I'll take your cases," said Mrs Ferris. "Follow me. I know we'll all be very happy together."

She bustled inside. Kurt and Inge stood together on the drive. Kurt took Inge's hand.

"Do come inside, children," called Mrs Ferris.

So they entered their new home together.

Mrs Ferris was wrong. They would never forget 'nasty old Hitler'. And they would never give up hope of seeing their parents either.

Kurt knew that getting used to living in England would be strange and hard.

Mrs Ferris was nice, but she didn't really understand. But, he resolved, they would get through.